MYSTERY OF THE WINDY MEADOW

Written by Ski Michaels
Illustrated by Allen Atkinson

Troll Associates

Library of Congress Cataloging in Publication Data

—

   Mystery of the windy meadow.

   Summary: When the meadow animals' things start dis-
appearing, Detective Duck searches for the thief.
   [1. Meadow animals—Fiction. 2. Mystery and detective
stories]   I. Atkinson, Allen, ill.   II. Title.
PZ7.P3656Myk   1986   [E]   85-14019
ISBN 0-8167-0630-1 (lib. bdg.)
ISBN 0-8167-0631-X (pbk.)

This edition published in 2002.

Copyright © 1986 by Troll Associates

Printed in the United States of America

10   9   8   7   6   5   4

MYSTERY OF THE WINDY MEADOW

Windy Meadow was a nice
place. It was open and wide
and filled with tall, green grass.
And it was always windy.

The meadow was a good place
to live.
"I like this meadow," said
Mr. Mole. "It is a good place
to read."
Mr. Mole always sat in the
meadow and read his
newspaper.

A meadow is a good place for a mouse. Mice like open, grassy places. Mrs. Mouse liked Windy Meadow. She liked to hang out her clothes to dry in the wind.

"Windy Meadow is a nice
place," said Mr. Beaver.
He liked to look for long, thin
sticks in the tall grass. There
were lots of long, thin sticks in
Windy Meadow.

Tim Turtle liked the open
meadow, too. He liked to look
for bits of string. Tim found lots
of string in Windy Meadow. He
made the bits into balls of
string.

Who else lived in the meadow?
Little Billy Bunny lived there.
Why did he like Windy Meadow?
Billy liked to fly kites. An open,
windy place is good for kite
flying.

One day something strange
happened in the meadow. Mr.
Mole was reading his newspaper.
He set the newspaper down in
the grass. He went away. When
he came back, the paper was
gone!

"Where is my newspaper?" asked
Mr. Mole.
He looked here. He looked there.
Mr. Mole looked and looked.
Did he find his paper? No!
"This is very mysterious," said
Mr. Mole.

"Quack! A mystery! Quack!
Quack!" called someone.
Out from the tall grass came a
strange-looking duck.
"I like mysteries," quacked the
duck. "Solving mysteries is what
I do best."

"Who are you?" asked Mr. Mole.
"I am Detective Duck," said the
stranger. "What has happened?"
Mr. Mole looked at Detective
Duck.
"My newspaper was there," he
said. "Now it is gone."

Detective Duck's tail wiggled.
His tail always wiggled when he
thought. And Detective Duck
was thinking.
"Maybe the wind took your
paper," he said. "Let's look in
the meadow."

Mr. Mole looked in the grass.
Detective Duck looked in the
grass. They did not see the
newspaper. It was not there.
It was gone. What a mystery!

Detective Duck's tail wiggled.
"The wind did not take the
paper," he said. "But someone
did. Who else lives in the
meadow?"

Mr. Mole thought.
"Mrs. Mouse and Mr. Beaver live here," he said. "Tim Turtle and Billy Bunny live here, too."
Detective Duck looked at Mr. Mole.
"Take me to Mrs. Mouse," he said.

Mr. Mole and Detective Duck
went to see Mrs. Mouse. Mrs.
Mouse looked upset.
"What is the matter?" asked Mr.
Mole.
"I was hanging out my
handkerchiefs to dry," said Mrs.
Mouse. "Then I went away.
Now they're gone!"

"That is strange," said Mr.
Mole.
"It is a mystery," said Mrs.
Mouse.
"Quack! It is a clue!" cried
Detective Duck.
And he wiggled his tail.

20

"Who is he?" Mrs. Mouse asked.
"He is Detective Duck," said
Mr. Mole. "He is looking for my
newspaper. He will look for
your handkerchiefs, too.
Detective Duck will solve this
mystery."

Detective Duck looked in the grass. He looked here. He looked there. There were no hankies to be seen. There were no clues.

"What do you think?" asked Mr.
Mole.
"I think someone took your
newspaper," Detective Duck
said. "And that same someone
took Mrs. Mouse's handkerchiefs."

Mr. Mole looked at Mrs. Mouse.
Mrs. Mouse looked at Mr. Mole.
"Who?" they asked. "Who did
it? And why?"

"I will find out," said the
detective.
He wiggled his tail.
"Take me to see Mr. Beaver," he
said.
"I will go too," said Mrs.
Mouse.
And away they went. They
went to look for Mr. Beaver.

They found Mr. Beaver in the
meadow grass.
"This is Detective Duck," said
Mr. Mole. "He is going to solve
a mystery."
"Good," said Mr. Beaver.
"Something strange happened to
me. Maybe you can solve my
mystery, too."

"What happened?" said
Detective Duck.
"Someone took my sticks," said
Mr. Beaver. "I put two long,
thin sticks in the grass. I went
away. Now the sticks are gone."

Mr. Beaver looked at Mrs.
Mouse. Mrs. Mouse looked at
Mr. Mole. Mr. Mole looked at
Detective Duck. What a mystery!

Gone was Mr. Mole's
newspaper. Gone were Mrs.
Mouse's hankies. Now Mr.
Beaver's sticks were gone, too.
Who took them? And why?

"Quack! I will look for clues,"
said Detective Duck.
He looked and looked.
"I see a clue!" he cried. "Look!"
And his tail wiggled and
wiggled.

What did he see? What was the
clue? It was a pot of glue.
"A pot of glue?" said Mr. Mole.
"That is a clue?" said Mrs.
Mouse.
"Some detective," said Mr.
Beaver.

"It is a clue," said Detective Duck. "And I am a good detective. I will solve this mystery. Take me to Tim Turtle."

Detective Duck took the pot of glue. And away they went into the meadow.

Tim Turtle was in the grass.
He was upset.
"Why are you upset?" asked Mr.
Beaver.
"Something strange happened,"
said Tim.
"What?" the others cried.

"I had some long string," said
Tim. "I made the long string
into a ball. I put the ball of
string in the grass."

Mr. Beaver looked at the grass.
Mr. Mole and Mrs. Mouse
looked, too.
"I do not see any string," said
Mr. Beaver.

"It is not there!" cried Tim Turtle. "I went away. When I came back, the string was gone!"

"Detective Duck will find your
string," said Mr. Beaver.
They all looked at the detective.

Detective Duck wiggled his tail.
He looked at the meadow. It
was very windy. It was a good
day for kite flying.

In the meadow was a little
bunny. The bunny had a kite.
The kite was high up in the air.
It was a very nice kite.

Detective Duck looked at the
kite. He looked at the glue.
"Newspaper, bits of cloth, and
thin sticks," he said. "And a ball
of string."
His tail wiggled and wiggled.

"Who is that?" asked Detective
Duck.

"That is little Billy Bunny," said
Mr. Mole.

"He lives in the meadow," said
Mrs. Mouse.

"Why do you ask?" said Mr.
Beaver.

"Come with me!" cried the
duck.
And away they went.

Detective Duck went up to Billy
Bunny.
"Is this your pot of glue?" asked
the detective.
Billy looked away from the kite
in the air. He looked at the
glue.
"It is!" Billy said.

"Quack! The mystery is solved!"
cried Detective Duck. "Billy
took the newspaper. He took the
handkerchiefs. He took the sticks
and ball of string."
Detective Duck went on.

"Billy made a kite. He glued the paper to the sticks. The hankies made a tail. The string is on the kite. The kite is in the air."

They all looked at Billy's kite.
"It *is* my newspaper," said Mr.
Mole.
"I see my sticks!" cried Mr.
Beaver.
"Those are my hankies," said
Mrs. Mouse.
"Can I fly the kite?" asked Tim
Turtle. "It is my ball of string."

Billy let Tim fly the kite.
"We can all fly the kite," he
said. "We all helped to make it.
I did not think anyone wanted
those things. I found them in
the meadow."

"QUACK!" said Detective Duck.
"The mystery of Windy Meadow
is solved!"